No Way, Wash Day

Written by
Adrienne Thurman

Illustrated by
Kaylani Juanita

HARPER
An Imprint of HarperCollinsPublishers

HarperCollins Children's Books, a division of HarperCollins Publishers,
195 Broadway, New York, NY 10007

HarperCollins Publishers, Macken House, 39/40 Mayor Street Upper,
Dublin 1, D01 C9W8, Ireland

No Way, Wash Day
Text copyright © 2026 by Adrienne Thurman
Illustrations copyright © 2026 by Kaylani Juanita
All rights reserved. Manufactured in Capriate San Gervasio, Italy.
No part of this book may be used or reproduced in any manner whatsoever without written permission except in the case of brief quotations embodied in critical articles and reviews. Without limiting the exclusive rights of any author, contributor, or the publisher of this publication, any unauthorized use of this publication to train generative artificial intelligence (AI) technologies is expressly prohibited. HarperCollins also exercises their rights under Article 4(3) of the Digital Single Market Directive 2019/790 and expressly reserves this publication from the text and data mining exception.
harpercollins.com

Library of Congress Control Number: 2025935885
ISBN 978-0-06-329005-1

The artist created the illustrations for this book digitally
along with scanned analog textures.
Typography by Dana Fritts
25 26 27 28 29   RTLO   10 9 8 7 6 5 4 3 2 1

First Edition

For Lyra . . . everything, always.

—A.T.

To all the tender-headed children
and those so scared of getting suds in their eyes
that they clench them until they see stars.

—K.J.

Nina Belle loved everything about her hair.

She loved the way it bopped and bounced to a funky beat.

She loved how it zigged and zagged to form ridges and valleys of a map that was all her own.

And she loved when it puffed and poofed like pom-poms to celebrate the game winning GOOOAAAAL!

Nina Belle loved everything about her hair.

Everything...
 except wash day.

It wasn't *always* so bad.

On some wash days, Mama hummed as she worked—fingers untying knots and gnarls like each strand was a precious thing.

"Have you ever seen a more perfect crown?" she'd ask. To which Nina would proudly reply, "Not ever."

But on other wash days, *most* wash days, Nina's troubles started long before her neck met the cold metal of the kitchen sink.

"Do I have to, Mama?"

When Mama's hands found her hips, Nina knew—mmmhmmm. She had to.

Luckily, Nina Belle was even more creative than her versatile hairdos. And she had plans of her own...

Maybe if Mama couldn't see it...
but Mama saw everything.

Maybe if she beat Mama to it...
but Mama wasn't having it.

After all, they had a schedule to keep.

But only if Mama could find her...

But with just one of *those* looks,
Nina knew she better try again.

"Please, Mama? Wash day is boring.
Wash day is painful. Wash day is—"

"Baby, wash day is *love*,"
Mama said, pulling Nina onto her lap.

"You know, when I was your age, I thought your Grams was tryin' to drown me in our old claw-foot tub. I'd plug my nose tight, like I was jumping off the high dive."

"But all those mornings, just me and Grams and the bubbles...
afternoons picking bows and beads and ball ties...
I wouldn't trade those wash days for anything.
It's the same now, but even better—"

"'Cause now you get to dunk me instead?" Nina asked.
Mama smiled. "Because now it's *our* time and *our* memories."

Nina Belle turned to Mama, and this time she was smiling too. "Still sounds like something we could do *tomorrow*."

Mama laughed, big and warm.

Today would be the *good* kind of wash day, and Nina Belle loved everything about that.

Well, almost everything...

Nina Belle's head fit perfectly in Mama's hands as she worked tiny bubbles into every curl.

Now, even when water flooded her face, or the part cut deep before Mama tugged a twist just a little too tight, Nina still felt like a precious thing.

"You know, someday you'll do this with your babies," Mama said, as she stacked Nina's hair high like a queen.

"Will you still do mine, Mama? Even then?"

"Even always."

"Don't forget to tip your stylist," Mama said with a wink.

So Nina Belle went in for a big old hug, because wash day is love.

And now she had one full week to figure out how to get out of the next one...